The Ten Commandments

~ FOR JEWISH CHILDREN ~

WRITTEN AND ILLUSTRATED BY

Miriam Nerlove

ALBERT WHITMAN & COMPANY

Morton Grove, Illinois

For Howard, with love.

My thanks to many, especially Sandy Kanter of Rosenblum's World of Judaica, Chicago;
Avi Averett, Ronit Ben-Arie, Jane Bobrick, Ruth Halpern, Cynthia Lerner, Holly Rosenberg,
and Irene Sufrin of the Solomon Schechter Day School, Skokie, Illinois; Rabbi Henry Balser;
and Abby Levine and Scott Piehl, for their invaluable help.

Also by Miriam Nerlove
Hanukkah & Passover & Purim & Shabbat

Library of Congress Cataloging-in-Publication Data

Nerlove, Miriam.
The Ten Commandments for Jewish children / written and illustrated by Miriam Nerlove.
p. cm.
Summary: Describes how Moses received the Ten Commandments,
what they contain, and how they should be obeyed.
ISBN 0-8075-7770-7
1. Ten commandments—Juvenile literature. [1. Ten commandments.] I. Title.
BM520.75N47 1999
296.3'6—dc21 99-10667
CIP

Text and illustrations copyright © 1999 by Miriam Nerlove.
Published in 1999 by Albert Whitman & Company,
6340 Oakton Street, Morton Grove, Illinois 60053-2723.
Published simultaneously in Canada
by General Publishing, Limited, Toronto.
Printed in the United States of America.

10 9 8 7 6 5 4 3 2 1

～ About the Ten Commandments ～

THE BIBLE tells us that almost four thousand years ago, and forty-nine days after the Israelites fled Egypt, God spoke to them at Mount Sinai. God talked to the Israelites through Moses and gave him the Ten Commandments on two stone tablets called the *luḥot ha-brit,* "tablets of the covenant."

The Israelites listened to the Ten Commandments and learned to live by them. These commandments became the first principles of their religion, which today is known as Judaism. People who follow the laws and traditional practices of Judaism are called Jews.

The Ten Commandments can be found in the Torah, which is a name for the first five books of the Hebrew Bible. They are first mentioned in the Book of Exodus and later in Deuteronomy. The commandments stress belief in the oneness of God. They tell the Jewish people to observe Shabbat, a day of rest. They include the most basic laws, such as not killing or stealing, that every society needs in order to survive in a just way.

The Ten Commandments set a foundation for a way of living. By following these rules we show respect for God and concern for the people and creatures around us.

A LONG TIME AGO, in the land of Egypt, the Israelites were slaves to a cruel pharaoh. They were unhappy and longed to be free.

God spoke to Moses, one of the Israelites, and told him to lead his people out of Egypt into the wilderness. God helped the Israelites, and Moses taught them to believe in the one God who had brought them out of Egypt.

One day, God told Moses to climb to the top of Mount Sinai. Moses stayed there for forty days and forty nights, receiving God's words, the Ten Commandments, which God wrote on two tablets of stone.

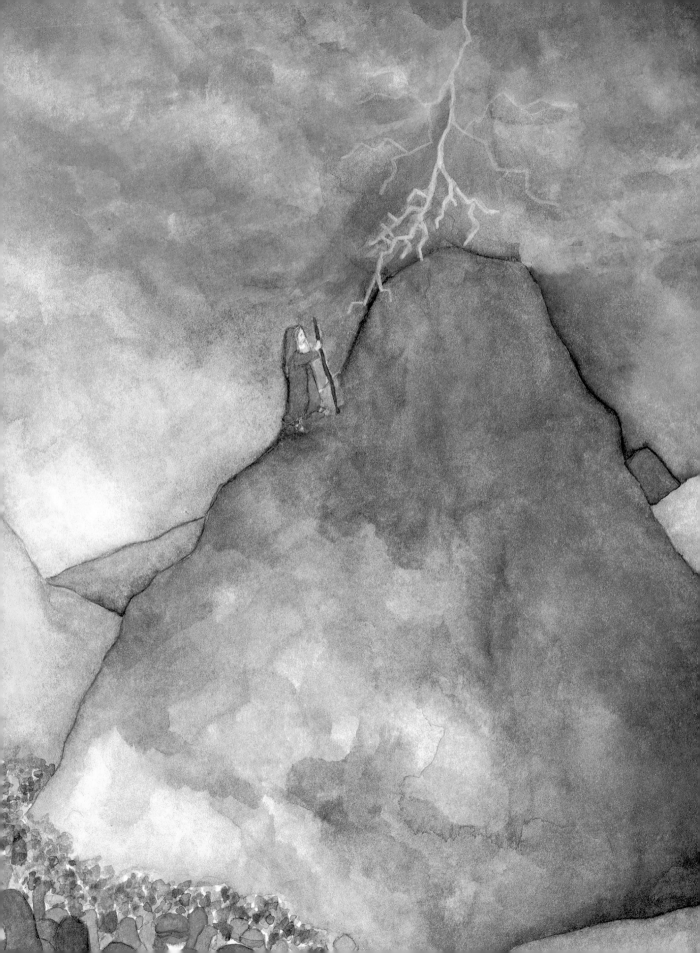

The Israelites grew afraid that Moses would not come back. They forgot their promise to believe in one God, and they melted their gold rings and bracelets to make an idol, a golden calf, to worship.

When Moses came down from the mountain, he saw the people singing and dancing around the golden calf. He was angry that they were worshiping an idol instead of God. Moses smashed the stone tablets and burned the golden calf.

Then Moses climbed back up the mountain to ask God to forgive them all. God did forgive them, and God gave the Ten Commandments again.

Returning, Moses read these commandments to the Israelites, who listened carefully. These are the Ten Commandments, the ten rules for living, that God wished the Israelites to follow.

I am the Lord your God.
I took you out of the land of Egypt,
out of the house of slavery.

Believe in one God, who has created all life.
Remember when the Jewish people were slaves in Egypt,
and remember that freedom is the right of all people.

You shall have no other gods except for Me.

Pray to only one God. There are no other gods
to be found in pictures, statues, or nature.

3

ג

You shall not use God's name with disrespect.

Don't misuse God's name,
and never use God's name to tell a lie.

Remember the Sabbath day
and keep it holy.

On Shabbat you are to rest and not work.
This is a day to pray and listen to the lessons of the Torah.
It is a good day for the family to be together.

Honor your father and mother.

Listen to your parents and learn from them.
Show them that you love them.
Help them when they need your help.

You shall not murder.

All living things are created by God.
Life should be respected.

You shall not be unfaithful to your husband or wife.

When two people marry, they promise God
and each other to love and be loyal for life.
They promise to share in life's hardships and blessings.

You shall not steal.

Respect other people's belongings,
and don't take what isn't yours.

You shall not make up stories about other people.

Don't say false or mean things about others.
Words can hurt people.

You shall not envy what belongs to others.

Work for what you want in life, and be glad for what you have.
Don't think a lot about what other people have.

1
I am the Lord your God.
I took you out of the land of Egypt,
out of the house of slavery.

2
You shall have no other
gods except for Me.

3
You shall not use God's
name with disrespect.

4
Remember the Sabbath day
and keep it holy.

5
Honor your father and mother.

6
You shall not
murder.

7
You shall not be unfaithful
to your husband or wife.

8
You shall not steal.

9
You shall not make up stories
about other people.

10
You shall not envy what
belongs to others.

The Israelites promised to follow the Ten Commandments.
"Na'aseh v'nishma!" they cried. "We shall do and obey!"

The Ten Commandments are wise rules for living. They are as important now as they were long ago, when Moses received them on the top of Mount Sinai.